THE
NEW
APOSTLES

And the legacy of Ishmael

PIERRIE MILLER

PALMETTO
PUBLISHING
Charleston, SC
www.PalmettoPublishing.com

Paperback ISBN: 9798822962743
eBook ISBN: 9798822962750

THE
NEW
APOSTLES

Contents

Introduction

When we are born, everything to us is new—the feeling of air biting our body to the sensation of our mother's or father's vibrations coming from their body into ours as they hold us against their bodies. What some will never realize and even more refuse to realize is that this connection starts way before we are thought of, before our own mother formed her ovaries or was even a thought, our connection to our parents is a very purposeful process. This concept may seem weird to some, (how can we select our parents?) but when looking into past life regressions and ancient spirituality, we find that our souls live far longer than we can ever imagine. And as our souls passed through the different dimensions of life their time of earth is spent learning and experiencing karma. Karma is popularly thought of as a funny colloquialism or saying, but it holds deeper meaning, and in some beliefs it not only connects to our whole being, but also the entire universe, so much so that our mere thoughts send a frequency or vibration out into the universe that effects every essence of who we are down to the smallest atom. Life on earth is but a mere initiation into the higher dimensions of reality, certain energies profit from humanity remaining unaware of this fact because the controllers powers have "discovered" (outside of outright slavery) that the best "way" to create a monetarily profitable society is to keep them in constant fear of loss, thus causing most to work harder to get out of this state, while those who are unable to are deemed useless or less deserving to society. How this plays into our soul connection is the fact that the constant grind to exist should not be a thing: a humanity existing of support and corporation is possible, and the sheer fact that this seems impossible to some is the proof that the controlling energies of this earth false chaos is prevailing. At some point in life (this life, or another) certain individuals tire of this process and awakens to the reality of what is happening on this planet, and slowly discovers the soul within their current existence in this human form. At this point in earth history, our soul, through many processes, selects it's parents to experience certain aspects of life that they either enjoyed or seek to improve to elevate their conscious out of this 3D prism that we experience here on earth. In this selection process, we accept all tasks that come before us knowing that everything is working as it should as our souls may have many lifetimes they are trying to commune with and heal. And as we are reborn through the water within our mother uterus and then pass through the vaginal cavity and into what we then known as our present heaven, and like a flash most of us will undergo a process of forgetting. This forgetting affects us all at different levels depending on the work we did during past lives. This leads us all to have different experiences on this planet as we are unaware who may have been in the past, and for this reason, if karma is taken into place, it is important to be conscious of your thoughts and actions, as they may have long-lasting results on others and yourself, and your future selves.

So, imagine, after undergoing the process of confusion and overall living to clear past karmic trauma, we are all born into this world passing the gates of our mother's uterus and entering the world, this four-dimensional space we call earth. For some of us, this is our first incarnation on this planet in human form, and for others of us who have yet to fully clear past karma, this could be our third time around trying to "get things right." The only other time in our current lives that we may experience this experience of birth is through the process of rebirth, and in this lifetime, rebirth can come as a change in thought pattern or having a new focus on self-care. The process of rebirth involves burning old ideas and patterns to make way for new varying ideas and experiences. In childhood, our imagination is our best friend, and in some cases, imaginary friends are even created by our imagination. Although we don't always experience the same experiences as children, the life of a child should be soft and supportive as a child learns lessons through experience and guidance. Life within this world is fast-paced and sometimes puts unnecessary constraints on parents when having children such that they are not able to provide the level of nurturing required for a child because of their own past traumas and self-doubts.

These children often undergo various versions of trauma, forcing them to grow and experience ideas beyond the normal teaching of individuals their age. These events coupled with each of our individual and soul personality formation leads to the way we see ourselves inwardly and express ourselves outwardly to others expressing itself as our own individual ego. . These personality types can be broken down into archetypes that can give a fishbowl lens view to certain common traits between individuals. Without knowing this, some of us have incarnated on this earth during a time when healing is needed, and without knowing it, we are healing the earth through our positive energy. This energy can be also called vibrations. In our own way we are all interconnected to earth's cosmic gird, and in a time of healing, the earth is undergoing a cosmic shift in which the cycle of reincarnation will come to an end as those individuals of a certain vibration will split from the energy maintaining the shell or veil over the 4D earth.

Some individuals in life understand that they have a higher calling and are known for portraying such characteristics that they have been deified. You can see these individuals as popular religious deities, saints and prophets. In this new age, there are many incarnated angels on this earth, and by reaching within, we have discovered life's initiations and discovered the true essence of our beings and discovered our truer purpose. I encourage those of you wondering what that uncertain tug to the universe is, those of you wondering why there is so much war and famine when the answer is right in front of us. For those individuals, this is your calling to lean into yourselves and seek "a deeper understanding, ask questions and seek" the deeper meaning to the things you see around you. As you learn to lean into your true self through different methods such as dream analysis, journaling, and meditation, you will discover your true purpose. We encourage you to keep walking the path and trust in yourself without fear of failure.

What is knowing? We grow up with the understanding that the people who we see above ourselves or give our power to in some way know more than we do about a specific thing or in a specific area. This is usually confirmed when that individual teaches you something either by example or by some sort of proof or example as to how it works or makes sense. Some of us, as we develop, begin to question this sense of knowing when we tell someone that we know something but are unable to provide the source or proof of the things we know. So at this point I may lose some individuals who have yet to experience events in a consistent manner that they have no choice but to question the current reality they live in. In these physical bodies that we live in, this can present itself as a sort of psychosis or stoicism, showing the range of diagnosis that can be attributed to those individuals who become confused by their own thoughts because they don't align with this feeling of knowing inside. This feeling of knowing may present itself differently in all individuals through the multi-faceted lives we are experiencing and have lived. Sometimes these senses of knowing come to us within; we may ask an internal question in our mind and suddenly see a flash in the corner of our eye that we discard as "something" or it could be a sudden response to a thought by something within our physical reality, such as a light flickering or an animal crossing. When we begin to pay attention to these things, we are able to realize that the universe is communicating with us in its own language.

The thought of this happening seems far-fetched to us in our current reality, but when we take a second and think, we may notice that we sometimes may be conscious of thinking while also having a concept of ourselves thinking about ourselves physically standing there conducting this process. Once we realize this, that thought is a conscious process, we begin to realize how much of a co-creator we are in the reality around us. As this knowledge of self begins to develop we start to realize that once impossible things are now seemingly possible within us all, but with this realization their also needs to be developed within us all the understanding of negative energy we are now aware of and capable of creating if we were to now move unconsciously about the earth. . So how do people do the impossible? They do this through knowing, not by believing or hoping or dreaming; this is done by knowing what is possible and aligning your own efforts or being in that direction with intent on goal accomplishment. As we do this throughout our lives, we might not notice when we do these things, but when we do notice,

Introduction

that builds awareness, and through that awareness you start to understand what manifestation is and begin to explore the depths of this path.

2154222222222222222

CHAPTER 1

Know Thyself

As Ishmael navigates through the challenges of his new life on earth, he discovers that he is not alone in his journey, through visions and sense responses, he has a sense of a bigger purpose for himself and his mission on earth. He eventually starts to decern talking patterns and personality traits often perceived as an anxios type are actually common characteristics of other spiritual beings who have also been sent down from the heavens to fulfill their destinies. Together, they form a powerful alliance, through insight and community consciousness, these individuals throughout the world use their gifts to protect the earth from dark forces that threaten to destroy it. Ishmael's powers continue to grow as he learns the nature of the elements and communicate with the spirits of the earth. He becomes a beacon of light in a world filled with darkness, inspiring others to embrace their own inner strength and potential, while at the same time placing a target on his back as the dark forces of this world have a far greater sight than most and also now can sense Ishmaels presence or essence even in his absence. The mere presence or thought of Ishmael can send a shock of energy radiating across the room disturbing some as they come to a sense of their own inner faults while also leaving others feeling inspired. But as Ishmael delves deeper into his mission, he uncovers a dark secret that threatens to unravel everything he has worked so hard to achieve. He must confront his own fears and doubts and make the ultimate sacrifice to save the world from destruction. These battles were not fault externally but within the soul of Ishmael himself as he must confront his inner most dark side and learn to integrate it into his new reality. At times during this battle he was looked at as insane, hypocritical, and an atheist. Ishmael was called everything but a saint, as the integration of one's own darkness can only truly be understood by those truly prepared for death. In the end, Ishmael emerges from seemingly a period of destitute victorious, his spirit stronger than ever before. As Ishmael continues to move about the earth more mysteries are revealed as he continues to meet more and more souls with the same flame lit within their inner being. As time passes he is eventually called back to the heavens, a hero and a legend, forever remembered for his courage and determination in the face of adversity. And so, the tale of Ishmael, the mystical warrior, lives on in the hearts and minds of all who hear his story, a reminder of the power that lies within each of us to overcome any obstacle and achieve greatness.

As Ishmael came to know himself more, he would internally be overwhelmed with joy, although externally, the world around him was crumbling. Attacks from various forces would attempt to penetrate his aura at every possible chance, from former friends and family to spiritual beings themselves, unconscious and conscious psychic attacks were attempted with an aim at derailing him from his mission and thrusting him once more into the great cycle of reincarnation. Often, these entities would utilize the deep-seated hurt that lies within every human as a catalyst to carry out their evil will.

Through all this, Ishmael struggles to maintain his sanity as his only friend no longer seems to understand the things that are suddenly very real in Ishmael's reality. Through trial and error, Ishmael put up his personal faculties to thwart the psychic attacks from the benevolent forces. Back down on earth, while remembering his soul contract and his purpose in this life, Ishmael's sense of feeling slowly became a sense of knowing.

Eventually, Ishmael would meet an earthly teacher. This teacher taught Ishmael to properly use his eye to see the world around him for what it truly is. Previously, in Ishmael's early lives, he had not truly used his vision to see. He often found himself caught up in long periods of self-doubt from the constant chastisement he received as a youth due to his eccentric personality and carefree attitude toward societal rules. Through diligent study, meditation, and guidance from his teachers, Ishmael was able to commit thousands of years of ancient text to memory through the use of vibrational wave forms. Instead of reading the text like a study manual, Ishmael would listen to the text read to him while also listening to music of a peculiar pitch in order to harness the vibrational coherence of the opposing sounds that will later sort themselves out in his mind.

As Ishmael navigates through the most unfathomable depths of this new world, he begins to discover he may just, in fact, be the savior he himself had always prayed for. With knowledge comes great responsibility, and although most of the world is unaware of the hidden threats that lie waiting beneath the earth, Ishmael lives beyond the vail and these beings are an ever present exists, waiting and biding their time like a Betelgeuse waiting for his name to be called. These entities become very aware of the presence of Ishmael in this world as his power begins to grow and they feel their grip on the world loosening.

As Ishmael's consciousness elevates, so do the powers of the beings that aim to throw him off track. His darkest thoughts begin to torment him for months on end, he often finds solace in his lustful encounters with a local priestess, Kafera. Their passion for one another is unmatched, but passion not focused on the right direction can lead to obsession. This was the case for Ishmael and the priestess. Together, they are powerful, and the magic they harness together can sometimes be so uncontrollable that they hurt themselves, trying to contain their true nature to one another. Kafera and Ishmael's story starts long before their present existence, although they suggest it between each other, they are equally unaware of their soul attachment. Tormented across every lifetime, Ishmael and his love once veiled to never to realize that they are one and the same, and fear is the only thing stopping them from exposing what they truly desire from one another—one looking to be loved, but afraid to wind up a widow, and Ishmael looking for family while walking a tightrope between heaven and hell. Their connection is a deeply spiritual one that started eons before our present era, in a time before separate sexes existed, Ishmael and Kafera were one being, an essence floating within the ether of Saturn, feeling nothing but love their senses were one, and as time passed they slowing evolved separately into their current existences, totally separate from one another.

Through this heartache and pain, Ishmael was able to break down barriers within himself and rebuild himself a new temple within, one that has been hardened by materialism and greed of the world, but also softened by the constant love flowing through his being. It is within this new temple that Ishmael became Ishmael the Sage. By mastering each sephirot within himself, the temple was built. Ishmael would often remind himself of the true nature of all those around him by reciting the following words;

This shell we call man is a complex being,
struggling to find balance and meaning.
We stumble and fall, but we rise again,
seeking to break free from the chains of sin.
They bind us down and hold us back,
a constant circle always on track.
Within a mirror, you will find,
not only yourself, but a soul as old as time.

Ishmael's Wish

The ego, a powerful force within,
Keeps us trapped in a cycle of sin.
It blinds us to the truth of our connection,
And fuels our sense of self-protection.
But deep within, there lies a spark,
A light that can pierce through the dark.
If we can let go of our ego's hold,
We can find unity, love, and gold.
So let us break free from the shell of man,
And embrace the oneness of all that we can.
Let us remember our true essence,
And live in harmony and presence.

CHAPTER 3

Ishmael's Fall

As Ishmael's power grew, so did the darkness that threatened to consume him. The evil forces that had been lurking in the shadows finally made their move, unleashing their full fury upon the earth. Ishmael and his fellow spiritual beings fought bravely, using all their powers to protect the innocent and defend the planet they had come to love.

But in the end, it was not enough. The darkness proved too strong, too relentless. One by one, Ishmael's allies fell, their light extinguished by the overwhelming force of evil. And in the final, fateful battle, Ishmael himself faced the ultimate sacrifice, not only giving all of his inner being, but also reaching a point physically were he could no longer out will those relentless entities surrounding him.

As he lay dying, surrounded by the devastation of the war, Ishmael looked up at the darkened sky. His heart heavy with sorrow, he knew that his time on earth was coming to an end. His mission had failed, his friends were gone, and he was powerless to stop the destruction that threatened to consume everything he had fought so hard to protect.

With his last breath, Ishmael whispered a prayer for forgiveness and peace for those who were unaware of his mission, and with all his being he set to one day return and correct his past imperfections. And as his spirit rose from his broken body, he felt a sense of release rush through his entire being. The burden of his duty lifted from his shoulders, he ascended into the heavens, leaving behind a world forever changed by his presence. Ishmael's tale ended in tragedy, his sacrifice a reminder of the harsh realities of life and the constant struggle between light and dark. But his legacy lived on, his memory forever etched in the hearts of those who had known him. And though he was gone, his spirit would continue to inspire others to fight for what is right, to never give up, and to always believe in the power of love and hope.

The presence of love was always with Ishmael and through the merger of the love between himself and Kafera, a child was born. A child a great potential with insight beyond her years. She came as an unexpected blessing to Kafera as she never was able to inform Ishmael of their joint creation. The child was golden in essence and her inner light shined just as her father's did, causing many outshoots of love into the atmosphere that once again disturbed those ruling souls who revel in the hysteria and confusion of the present era. The child named Indigo would eventually be sought after by those who know her lineage and potential

and would be forced to be placed outside of society to protect her blood born right.

Although these are new beginnings for some, Ishmaels
end was inevitable, finding peace in the knowledge that he had
done all he could, that he had fought with all his strength, and
that he had lived and died for a cause greater than himself.
Still remembered as a strange wondering soul to some, Ishamel
wisdom and gifts spoke for themselves, earning him the title of
Ishmael the Sage, although from the mouths of those without
the ability to embrace purity, he is still referred to as a more
dark an ominous being. This appearance of Ishmael as a negative being was not done unintentionally, as the awareness of his
legacy spread throughout the world, more and more individuals embodied the essence of Ishmael often being overwhelmed
by a feeling of inspiration and love at the mere mention of his
name. With fear that he could possibly have an offspring who
may harness the same divine spark within them, the energies of
chaos spread throughout the earth in a mystical battle within
the inner being of those individuals who had yet to understand
the story of Ishmael. Those individuals received dreams of a
man who claimed to be a gift from the heavens, but upon his
lifetime on earth, the earth dove deeper into chaos due to his
extreme society views and lack of authority causing worldwide
distrust and disfunction. In their dreams these individuals em-
body the truth of this individual. He would come to be called
by these sleepers, Damon the destroyer. Unaware of the true
personality of Ishmael, Damon had now been attributed to

the good and the bad deeds of Ishmael as a type of evil archi-type who chose to go against the ruling authorities only to end up cast off into the depth of nothingness. Still caught in the time of remembering Ishmaels spirit soared among the stars, he knew that his journey was not over, that he would live on in the cosmos, a beacon of light in the vast darkness of the universe, a demon to some and an angle to others. With this fate, Ishmaels floats above the earth pouring down light into all those beings capable of receiving it.

CHAPTER 4

The Legacy of Ishmael

The sun was setting on the battlefield, casting a golden hue over the blood-soaked ground where the fallen lay. Ishmael, the ethereal being who had taken on human form to guide and protect his people, lay mortally wounded at the heart of the battlefield. His physical body, once strong and noble, was now broken and fragile.

As Ishmael's life force slowly ebbed away, he felt a profound sense of sadness wash over him. His mission, his purpose, had been cut short. He had tried to lead his people to victory, to inspire them to rise against the tyranny of their oppressors. But now, as he lay dying, he knew that his efforts had been in vain.

Already departed from his body, memories flashed before his eyes—the faces of his comrades, the battles they had fought together, the courage and sacrifice that had defined their struggle seems to only be like a grain of sand in the ocean, as he realizes the vast nature of the universe and his true mission on earth. And yet, Ishmael can only wonder why, despite all their bravery, they had been outnumbered and outmatched. The nature of the universe is one that can never be truly understood, and the purpose and process of death will forever be a mystery to some, and an even bigger mystery to those who live in fear. Why would the universe allow death to befall such an important person? It was obvious the enemy's forces had been too great, too powerful, and too well organized for the battle to truly be fought on the battlefield. But as Ishmael's consciousness began to fade, he felt a strange sense of peace wash over him. He knew that his physical body may be gone, but his spirit would live on. The memory of all his good deeds and efforts to uplift his people would awaken a flame within the hearts of those who had witnessed his sacrifice.

And true to his final thoughts, a change began to sweep across the land. The people, inspired by Ishmael's example, began to question the establishment, to fight against the forces of oppression and injustice. The world was transformed as science and religion came together through metaphysical studies such as those within theosophy, anthroposophy, and quantum physics, bridging the gap between the material and the spiritual worlds in a way that can no longer be denied.

Over time magic became a reality to humanity as the stories of Ishmael and Damon begin to reach every corner of the earth and his mystical abilities are slowly discussed in higher institutions of education and amongst the most common folk. The stories of his offspring begin to circulate and over a matter of decades, more and more stories are spread of his descendants and their divine gifts. Although magic becomes openly talked about and understood, there are still only a few individuals who truly practice and understand this natural ability that is a true power within all of us that connects us to the world around us. With their energy high, they accomplished feats that once seemed impossible. The consciousness of Ishmael lived on, a beacon of hope and inspiration, guiding the people toward a brighter future, while also bellowing below the surface of reality was the darker character of Ishmael 'Damon' and the forces that stand behind him proclaiming his divine evil at times and others calling for his resurrection to return to a time when the earth was unaware of magic and more "free will" existed throughout the earth.

But as time passed, memories faded, and the people began to forget the sacrifices that had been made. The heroism of Ishmael the Sage became a legend, a fable told to children as they drifted off to sleep. The world slipped back into chaos, the people blinded by their own desires and fears.

As Ishmael's spirit watched from beyond, like a silent observer he watched the world fall into darkness once more. The memory of his noble sacrifice faded away from some of his strongest followers, and the books containing his wisdom became outlawed and lost in time, so did the oral teachings, all lost to the annals of time as the people succumbed to their own worst instincts.

But deep within the hearts of a few, the memory of Ishmael lived on. And though the world may have forgotten the true purpose of life on the earth, those few who have ears to hear the call have chosen to carry his legacy forward by faith alone, a glimmer of hope in the face of despair, not quiet knowing their end goal, but with their inner most being they are willed to do great things. Within these individuals lies that same spark that combust within Ishmael at a young age, but this new age of men were born with the spark, this trait began to manifest itself outwardly and thus these individuals became outwardly identifiable. The trait characterized or called the spart presented itself as a cluster of freckles located somewhere on each individuals face, hands or neck that resemble the star formation from the time of their birth. These individuals, although gifted, within them exist a sense of I, and if their gifts remain unharnessed there existence on Earth can be weaponized for the product of evil. Thus so, as evil lay at bay, waiting for its moment to strike once more, the spirit of Ishmael the Sage would watch over the world, as a silent guardian in the shadows of history.

CHAPTER 5

Rebirth as a Seer

The Legacy of the Seer:
Embracing the Magic of Existence

I n the land of Eldoria, there existed a prophecy foretelling the arrival of a reincarnated priestess who would hold the key to unlocking the mysteries of the universe. Indigo was a young woman who found herself thrust into this magical world, unaware of her true destiny. After what seemed to be a lifetime of travel from land to land having to hide her identity, she always new she was important, but to her she was just another child of the universe, just as those around her. Over the years of her travel's indigo developed a great ability to decern wrong from right and would often intimidate individuals because of her ability to sense the deeper understanding of the words, symbols and sounds around her. These often led to deeper relationships with those with good intentions, but while when in contact with individuals who may have a more selfish nature it creates a disturbance within them causing her individual light to reflect the darkness of the individual back to them. Most men at this time were of a selfish nature, as the concept and knowledge is known this only led to more ambitious men attempting to harness and control the universal elements. Indigo's ability to SEE has aided her in coping with her everchanging surroundings, while also stunting her personal development for true friendships. The land of Eldoria seemed to feel different from the lands she visited in the past. In this land existed a unique tapestry of being ranging from fairies, nymphs, salamanders, and phantoms. Each being having their own essence while also maintaining a group consciousness that allows them to geer their work towards a common objective. The individual personalities can not be taken as good or bad, as their sole mission is the protection of the mineral world around them.

As Indigo navigated the lush forests and towering mountains of Eldoria, she discovered that she possessed a unique ability to communicate with the ancient spirits that dwelled within the land. These spirits guided her on her quest to uncover the secrets of her past life as a powerful priestess who had once communed with the gods themselves. Just like the ascended masters and great sages of the past Indigo must also undergo a death and rebirth as she discovers the nature of her true being. The process of knowing one's self is a difficult process in it's own right, but to know yourself and have full awareness of your past lives is a unique gift, that when combined with pure love, can overcome any amount of evil, and cements the individuals space in time, accentually becoming immortal to the death process as death only exists in the realm of fear based realities.

While the land of Eldoria was a magical land that was very beautiful to behold. The land a vast with lush green fields, snowcapped mountains and crystalline structures seemed to be a dreamworld to people who had heard of its beauty, and for some select individuals of Earth they often dream of this place unknowingly connecting to a parallel reality of their own, not separate from them, but vibrationally different, which in a dream state their bodies were able to enter this seemingly astral world. Eldoria lies within the same physical space as Earth, but behind the vail that clouds our Earthly vision from the forms and beings that lie outside Earths base vibration. The beings of Earth are unaware of their density as it relates to physical matter, and it is this exact density that one must shed itself of to grasp the reality of the etheric world around them. At this present moment Eldoria has been inhabited by all sorts of beings, magical, non-magical, gifted individual who have been granted vision to SEE the world, and those black magician who by nefarious means have opened doorways to this other world they so long to SEE. This is done by the harnessing of dark powers through a unique combination of chemicals and chants that would lift their consciousness out of the dark. For those individuals this is a very limited experience as their constant need for essence leads them to falling back down into the normal states of reality. The presence of these "magical" Earth humans is new to the inhabitants of Eldoria, as their presence has brought a dark energy to the land of Eldoria, the establishment of kings, judges, and provinces have been enacted across the land. Although a very real concept of Earth, this concept did not exist within Eldoria, the beings of Eldoria are one with nature and do not see separateness from themselves and the living ground and world around them. This thought lived within the fiber of the beings of Eldoria and in such they operated under a group consciousness always aimed at bettering the world around them. With this being ingrained in them down to the smallest atom of their essence, they had never had a need for a leader, laws, or separate land. The health of all was placed before personal needs and gain. They could not operate any differently as the universe speaks to these beings directly guiding their daily activities as if under a trance from a higher power.

Since the fall of Ishmael there has been rumors that their lived Earth born humans of his decent that also possess the understanding of the world and are indeed blessed by the gods themselves with divine wisdom and knowledge. This wisdom combined with a unselfish heart has the ability to challenge every worldly aspect of life that aims to hold individuals back from their true essence of being. The danger of this since of self would crumble the churches and kingdoms of the world as individuals awaken to their own divinity and connected to the All. Individuals with this knowledge would be as demi-gods on earth as their wisdom surpasses common science, as it is based on experience and mysticism that most people call myth. The lineage of Ishmeal have been hunted in recent years and these gifted children were intentionally spread across the globe, often having to hide their true identity taking seemingly humble positions in society. For those few such as Indigo their inner glow is so bright, that even with constant movement and discuses, their inner nature can still be sensed by certain gifted individuals, for this reason Indigo could never stay in one place for too long, as her presence alone attracts energy in both positive and negative ways as individuals come within her vicinity. Some of Ishmael's offspring that were especially gifted simply disembarked this Earth, akin to a physical death but for these souls, there internal powers far surpassed their physical bodies which would lead to their eventual passing on from this Earth, often by their own choice.

These children were gifted beyond all measure, a testament to this fact that the boiling want and need for these children eventually lead to their capture and killing throughout the lands where they were discovered. This turned out to be the most disastrous things for those dark forces within nature, as the Universe governs the earth and the lords of the earth can not destroy the lives of divine beings, and as a law these beings are always reborn at another point in time to deliver the same message, thus continuing the fight for the stability of Earth. Damon sought to put people in power that he controlled through their own likes, as their individuals' personalities already held an essence of the seed of Damon, so around and within these individuals existed a atomic seed, of selfishness. Depending on how often these individuals' water that specific seed it may lead them to great accomplishments and therefore they are blessed with knowledge, this knowledge is of a mechanical nature, and this knowledge is a blessing from Damon as they only do his bidding the more these individuals shift away from the natural magic of the universe. This promoted these individuals to lead down very selfish paths in the name of bettering humanity, thus trapping lost souls in a never-ending materialistic reality that only aims to divide and separate humanity from their eternal home within the stars.

These men and women who held the seed of Damon within them, specifically those who used the harnessing of magical essence to enter into different vibrational planes, these individuals beings guided by Damon sought to enter relationships with those pure souls in order to create mix blood offspring who posses the ability to operate within both polarities of the magical essence being able to walk between the heavens and the hells as a faithful warrior to the side they chose to serve. A soul of this power and type is especially dangerous as they could penetrate any realm and world place in front of them as a blockage on their path. An individual with this power, working for self could cause great destruction throughout the land. In fables of the past this individual would be called the Anti-Christ. Causing such devastation to the world as the long-forgotten inhabitants of the lands of Lemuria.

With each step she took, Indigo felt a deep connection to the world around her, as if the very essence of the universe pulsed through her veins. She encountered mystical creatures and faced formidable challenges that would cause her to question herself and her abilities but her determination never wavered as she relied on her memory of the stories of Ishmael and his great deeds as a human on earth was known to walk with God. Often reciting Ishmaels prayer as mantra she knew that her journey was not just for herself, but for the greater good of Eldoria, the planet and all who inhabited it.

Along the way, Indigo met a band of loyal companions who joined her on her quest. There was Renn, a fearless warrior with a heart of gold; Luna, a wise healer who could mend both body and soul; and Orion, a mischievous bard whose songs could lift even the heaviest of spirits. Together, they formed an unstoppable team, united in their goal to protect Eldoria from the forces of darkness that threatened to consume it. Unlike Indigo, her fellow warriors have always been outwardly magical as they have never known anything other than natural beings of Eldoria. Together they can accomplish much but each individually is hunted by their own unique darker half. We must always remind ourselves of the nature of Eldoria, although the joint goal is peace throughout the land, even the purest beings have a since of ego that effects the means at which they want to accomplish this task.

As they ventured deeper into the heart of Eldoria, Indigo and her companions uncovered ancient ruins and hidden temples that held clues to the priestess's past. These places and locations are known to few, even within Eldoria only as myth do, they exist to some, as they are either unbelieving or not able to SEE the signs that lead to the greatest mysteries. Each revelation brought them closer to unlocking the true power that lay dormant within Indigo, waiting to be unleashed. There was one within the group who could see Indigos soul, this was Orion, also a old soul from the Saturn carnation. He understands the nature and importance of Indigos being, but his selfish behavior acts as a block from him truly realizing that when in the presence of Indigo, he at times may be speaking with an ascended master possessing the consciousness of the Christ.

But their journey was not without its challenges. At times personalities would clash as frustration would set in during the most arduous portions of their journey. Renn, a warrior by nature, would often go out ahead of the others to scout the land and prided himself on takin the lead, often facing the most formidable foes alone. This was not an issue until Renn's faith in himself started to waver after an extremely hard-fought battle where he suffered a leg injury that has ceased to heal properly. They faced treacherous obstacles and cunning adversaries who sought to thwart their progress at every turn. Luna, sensing Renn's self-doubt offered to aid in his healing. With his consent Luna gathered materials from within the earth to apply to Renn's wound, through the power of thought and focused speech Luna harnessed the healing essence and released it upon Reen's wound. With wide eyes Renn was astonished to see his wound gradually healing itself. With each trial they overcame, Indigo grew stronger and more attuned to the magic that flowed through her.

With darkness slowly taking hold of the beings of Eldoria Indigo's mission met hurdle after hurdle as her and her companions have come under the eye of one of the darkest wizards known to man. This wizard has been unheard of for centuries, but through the efforts of those faithful individuals praising the deity of Daimon. The praises for this dark energy grew and grew through dark powers; by amassing enough essence from those gifted children these dark wizards were able to raise their leader Daimon from the dead. With his own mission in mind, he has set out to stop Indigo from fulfilling her destiny. Now running for their lives while trying to keep their inner faith they eventually felt themselves getting closer to their destination. After many long and arduous months of travel, Indigo and her companions reached the summit of Mount Celestia, where the final piece of the puzzle awaited them. There, at the peak of the mountain, they found a sacred altar bathed in the light of a thousand stars, pulsing with the energy of creation itself. The energy of this place seemed to work wonders on the souls of those individuals who stepped within the mountain. The reality of their past and current lives was revealed to them and each individual was endowed with full awareness of their true place in this universe.

As Indigo stepped forward and placed her hands upon the altar, a blinding light enveloped her, filling her with a sense of peace and purpose unlike anything she had ever known. In that moment, she remembered who she truly was: a priestess of the highest order, chosen to bridge the gap between the mortal realm and the divine.

With a surge of power that shook the very foundations of Eldoria, Indigo unleashed a wave of energy that cleansed the land of all darkness and despair. The skies cleared, the sun shone brightly, and the people of Eldoria rejoiced, knowing that their savior had arrived.

In the days that followed, Indigo took her place as the spiritual leader of Eldoria, guiding its people with wisdom and compassion. The land prospered under her reign, and peace reigned once more in the realm.

As she looked out over the kingdom, she now called home, Indigo knew that her journey was far from over. The mysteries of the universe still beckoned to her, calling her to explore new realms and unlock even greater potentials. But she also knew that she was exactly where she was meant to be, surrounded by friends who had become family, and a world that had embraced her as its own. So, with a heart full of gratitude and a spirit ablaze with possibility, Indigo set out on her next great adventure, knowing that whatever trials lay ahead, she would face them with courage, grace, and the knowledge that she was truly a divine entity sent on an impossible mission.

But still within the unseen now lies the ether and at times physical existence of Damon and his worldly stewards lying wait, ruling as lords of illusions hypnotizing the masses, slowly building an army large enough to manifest an energy so divisive that a final call will be made for those truly forgetful souls that long for the most deviant types of connections. The polarity's of reality will always out way any future predictions, so we can only allow things to be as they are and maintain and let our hopes lie in the story of Ishmael as this alternate future could someday be a future of our own.

About the Author

Pierrie Miller, author of The New Apostles, is a devoted explorer of the metaphysical realm. His fascination with what is deemed unique or peculiar by others has evolved into a fervent desire to write. This allows him to articulate the ideas of predecessors, intertwined with his own unique perspectives. Miller's work offers a refreshing dive into the mystical, appealing to those intrigued by spirituality and the occult. With a writing style that resonates with young adults and older teenagers, his passion and dedication shine through his words, making him an enchanting voice in the world of metaphysical literature.

Milton Keynes UK
Ingram Content Group UK Ltd.
UKHW030919121124
451094UK00005B/373